DEC 2019

W9-BRL-510

RAIN MAKES APPLESAUCE

Appreciation by Jerry Pinkney

I first read *Rain Makes Applesauce* three years out of art school, shortly after designing and illustrating my first picture book, *The Adventures of Spider* by Joyce Cooper Arkhurst. The process of illustrating *Spider* captured my imagination in a way I had not expected and I was hooked. Bookmaking emerged as the new direction and focus of my career.

When I shared this with a fellow artist, he introduced me to four books that would change and shape how I pursued my vision of bookmaking until this very day: *The Wonder Clock*, written and illustrated by Howard Pyle; *The Wind in the Willows*, written by Kenneth Grahame and illustrated by Arthur Rackham; *The Honeybees*, written by Franklin Russell and illustrated by Colette Portal; and most importantly, *Rain Makes Applesauce*, written by Julian Scheer and illustrated by Marvin Bileck. I cherished these publications, fearing I might just wear out the pages.

Over the years, these books have taken their place on my shelves among other classics I have collected. However, it was Julian Scheer's delicious and poetic text and Marvin Bileck's stunning illustrations that I returned to time and time again for inspiration. Bileck's line, expressively nuanced, held so much power. His pastel palette added warmth to the overall feel of his vignettes. His art was rich in humor in the tradition of Pieter Bruegel the Elder's drawings and prints, and lyrical in the way of Carl Larsson's paintings. Bileck's art nourished and fed my own, acting as a high-water mark for what I desired to achieve in bookmaking. *It's not impossible for Marvin,* I'd think when I hit a roadblock and referred back to *Rain Makes Applesauce*. It is bookmaking at its best—an extraordinary knitting of text and art that stands the test of time.

To Susan, Scott, and Grey
and in memory of Leslie

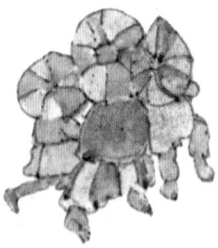

Text copyright © 1964 by Julian Scheer • Art copyright © 1964 by Marvin Bileck
Introduction copyright © 2019 by Jerry Pinkney • All Rights Reserved
HOLIDAY HOUSE is registered in the U.S. Patent and Trademark Office.
Printed and bound in April 2019 at Tien Wah Press, Johor Bahru, Johor, Malaysia
www.holidayhouse.com • First Edition
1 3 5 7 9 10 8 6 4 2

ISBN: 978-0-8234-0091-1 (hardcover)
ISBN: 978-0-8234-4361-1 (restored hardcover edition)

CHARLESTON COUNTY LIBRARY

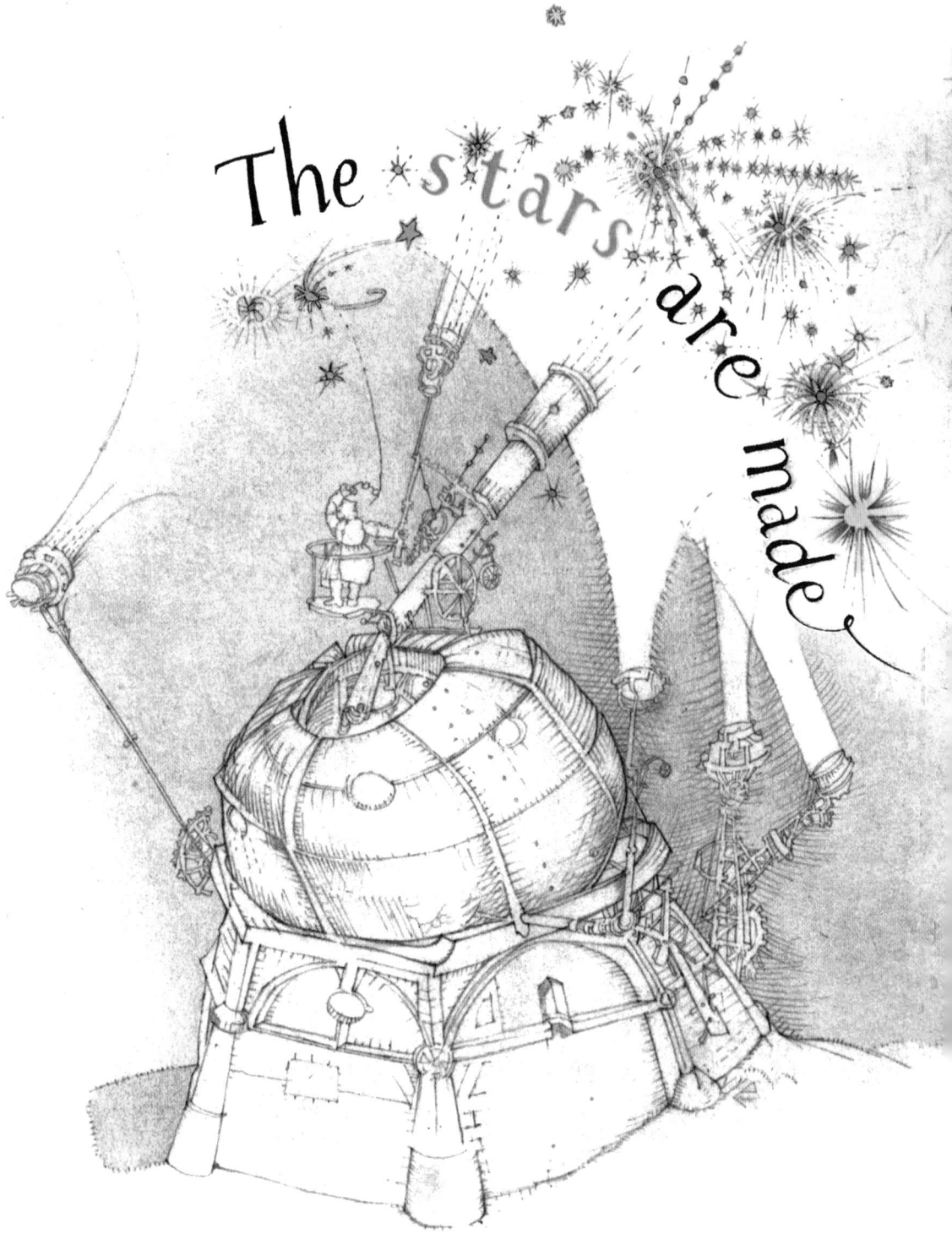
The stars are made

of lemon Juice
APPLE SEED
MARY
and rain makes applesauce
oh you're just talking silly talk

I wear my shoes

inside out
and
rain makes
applesauce

My house goes walking

every day
and
rain
makes
apple sauce
Oh you're
just talking
silly talk

Dolls go dancing

on the moon
and
rain makes applesauce

The wind blows
backwards
all night

long
and
Oh you're just talking silly talk
makes applesauce

Monkeys mumble

in a jelly bean jungle
and
rain makes applesauce

Candy tastes like
CANDY
WORKS
Chew DOUBLE TROUBLE GUM
DANDY CANDY

soap soap soap
and
rain and applesauce
OH YOU'RE JUST TALKING SILLY TALK

Monkeys eat

the chimney smoke and

Tigers sleep on an elephant's
and
rain makes applesauce
oh
you're

snoot
just talking
silly
talk

Clouds hide in

a hole in the sky
and
rain
makes
applesauce

Salmon slide
down a Hippo's hide

and rain makes applesauce

My Teddy Bear sings out

loud at night
and
rain makes applesauce

FUNNYBONE
A.C.
MEMBERS
ONLY
Elbows
grow

on a tickle tree
and
rain
makes applesauce

Oh, you're just talking silly, silly talk.

I know I'm
talking
silly talk...
But-

Rain makes
NUT
SUGA
MEG
The Sea of Applesauce

apple·sauce